BEAUTY AND THE BEAST

A CHRISTMAS REGENCY ROMANCE

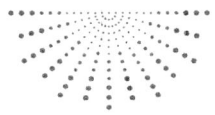

CHARITY MCCOLL

Publisher's Note: This is a work of fiction. Names, characters, places, and incidents are a product of the author's imagination. Locales and public names are sometimes used for atmospheric purposes. Any resemblance to actual people, living or dead, or to businesses, companies, events, institutions, or locales is completely coincidental.

© 2019 PUREREAD LTD

PUREREAD.COM

CONTENTS

Prologue	1
1. Facing Life	5
2. The Yearning Heart	12
3. The Unexpected Guest	20
4. Through the Wall	28
5. Bright Night	38
6. A Changed Man	56
7. Is This Love	61
8. Love at Last	68
Epilogue	72
Our Gift To You	77

PROLOGUE

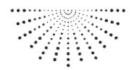

S*pring 1815*

"*From dust to dust,*" *the old vicar's voice droned on and Ariel Dixon stared at the wooden coffin that was being lowered into the gaping hole in the earth.* "*From the earth you came, Margaret Dixon, and to the earth we return your mortal body, to await the resurrection of the saints.*"

Ariel looked around the cemetery. Her mother had been a well-loved woman, always welcoming everyone with a big smile on her face. No one was considered a stranger by Margaret, and she'd always treated everyone with kindness and respect.

The small cemetery was packed with mourners who all had only good things to say about the dead woman. It all looked surreal, and Ariel's glance rested on her father, whose heaving shoulders told her that he was still weeping for his lost love. He'd not stopped crying from the moment the doctor pronounced her mother dead two days ago. What had started out as a mild headache had soon developed into a cough that wouldn't stop, and Margaret had soon collapsed. She slipped into unconsciousness and never woke up. Hours later, she was dead.

That her parents had loved each other so deeply was obvious in the way there had always been laughter in their home. Even though her father was a mere blacksmith and her mother a seamstress and their fare was small, yet their home had always been filled with laughter and love.

"Ariel," her mother had once told her, "It's not material wealth that makes for a happy home. What is in here," she touched her heart, "Is what makes a home a loving one. Your father and I didn't have much when we met, and even now, life is still a struggle. But we have each other, and you our beautiful daughter."

"Mama, when I grow up, I'll marry a rich prince and then you and Papa can come and live with us in our palace," Ariel said.

"My darling, it isn't riches that will bring you joy. Ariel, if you meet a simple and humble man who loves you, don't reject him because he isn't rich. There's no wealth in the

world like that of a peaceful home that is filled with laughter and happiness. Always remember that."

Ariel could still hear her mother's sweet voice telling her to be strong for her father. She didn't want to believe that she would never behold her mother's beautiful face again. Never sing hymns tunelessly with her and all the while both of them giggling like two small children. Or hear her father lovingly admonishing them for terrifying the birds off the trees with their terrible singing. The three of them would then collapse into laughter, and to Ariel, her simple life had been perfect.

Now all that was gone forever, and when the first spade of earth hit the coffin with a dull thud, she screamed.

"No, stop!" She tried to run to the graveside, intending to jump in, but strong hands held her back. "Mama, please come back to us," she sobbed in anguish, and the dam finally burst open. Ariel hadn't shed a single tear when the doctor pronounced her mother dead. Nor had she cried when the embalmers came to the house and disappeared into her parents' bedroom to prepare her mother's body for burial. Nor had she cried as she followed the pall bearers into the church and then to the graveside, refusing to accept that her mother was really gone.

But it all came pouring out now. The reality of what had happened finally hit her and the seventeen-year-old girl was inconsolable.

"God will take care of you," were the words whispered to her over and over again, and she wanted to scream harder. Where was God when her mother had suddenly fallen ill and then left them?

1
FACING LIFE

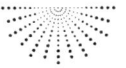

W*inter – 1815*

"Pa, I'm going out now," Ariel looked at her father who was seated on the frayed couch in front of a fire that was dying down in the grate. "I've brought some wood in, so the fire won't die down. I'm going to find us some deer or hare for dinner. Maybe I'll even shoot a fat duck for our Christmas Day dinner in two days' time," she tried to joke but it fell flat.

Her father man sat silently through the conversation, taking an occasional sip from the whiskey bottle that was in his hand. It was the very cheap kind of liquor and smelled terrible. But Arthur Dixon didn't care at all. It at least numbed his senses, and he didn't have to think about the woman he'd loved for nineteen years and lost last spring.

Ariel twisted her lips and sighed, picking up her sling and small satchel bag that contained nicely rounded pebbles chosen carefully from the brook just a few yards from their little cottage.

She had kept the family going for the past eight months and she felt like she was reaching her breaking point. But she'd made her mother a promise that she would take care of her father. Even if he pretty much ignored her most of the time and didn't care if she ate or slept hungry. His drinking was getting worse by the day, and her greatest fear was him one day being found dead in a ditch somewhere. Even a drunk father was better than being left as an orphan and all alone.

As she walked out of their two-bedroom cottage, she turned back for a last glance at her father.

"Pa, please be careful. I'll be back as soon as I can to prepare something for us to eat."

The only response she got was a grunt and the raising of the half-filled bottle to his lips. Ariel felt really sad. This was going to be the first Christmas without her mother, and she knew her father was drinking himself into a stupor so he could forget his pain.

"But what about me," she wanted to scream at the unfairness of it all. Her father had his strong drinks to help numb his pain, but what about her? Who would take away the pain she was feeling?

In past years, at such a time like this, their house would have a small fir tree that would be decorated with scraps of colourful material left over from customers' gowns. The house would be filled with the warm and pleasant aroma of ginger cookies and pies. Her father would go out and return with one or two ducks, which her mother would then dress with herbs grown in the small garden behind their cottage.

The garden was now covered in snow and Ariel didn't think she would ever work in it again. The memories of the time spent out there with her mother were too raw and painful. It was while they were working together that her mother would give her words of wisdom about life, and Ariel missed all that. In the months after her mother's death, she'd sold the herbs that had still been growing in the garden so they could have food on the table. But she refused to continue cultivating it, and it had soon become overrun with weeds.

Wiping the tears from her eyes, she made her way to the path that led into the thick woods that were a short distance from the house. Her father wouldn't miss her for a while, but she intended to return soon and think about what they were going to do for Christmas.

From when she could walk and follow her father around, he'd started taking her hunting with him whenever her mother permitted it. And there weren't many things that Margaret permitted her husband to teach their little girl. From the way her father treated her, it was clear that he'd longed for a male child, and so whatever skills he had, he'd imparted to her.

With time, she became so skilled at hunting that people started calling her the Great Huntress of Berkeley. And she loved her nickname because it denoted everything she loved. From climbing trees in the woods to pick wild fruit so her mother could make them jam and pudding, to fishing for trout in the stream, Ariel did them all. And while her mother had protested that a young girl should be taught how to keep house and home, her father was very proud of her achievements.

Ariel smiled in fond remembrance as she plunged into the thick woods, using a stick she'd picked up to clear a path for herself. Though the air was chilly, Ariel ignored the cold and walked on, her old boots making a squishing sound as they crunched the snow beneath her feet. The sun was up and most of the snow had melted, which meant that the pond would have some ducks swimming on it, hoping to catch a fish or some snails. There wasn't much game to be found in winter, but she was sure of shooting one or two ducks. That would tide them over until Christmas Day.

But they had also run low on other essential foodstuff, and she needed to catch a few more animals or birds to sell. And then the rent was also due at the end of the year. Just thinking about the obligations that she had to meet before the year ended filled her with dismay.

When her mother was still alive, her parents had barely managed to scrape by and now that her father did nothing other than drink whatever wages he got from his job, it was left to her to ensure that they never went hungry and that the rent was paid in good time.

Their cottage was part of a baron's estate, and the nobleman, though absent from his seat for most of the year, had someone managing the place for him. Which meant that the caretaker had to collect the rents, and he was a tough man who didn't accept any excuses. And Ariel always made sure she had the rent so the man would take it and leave. He always made her feel uncomfortable whenever he came around, and many times she wished her father would be in his right senses so he could put the man off from ogling her so shamelessly.

Ariel glanced up at the trees that loomed above her. Droplets of snow hanging at the ends of leaves glimmered in the sunshine like small diamonds. She longed for the father she had loved to return and be the man he used to be. The man who would swing her up in the air and hoist her onto his shoulder as she laughed giddily, while her mother watched them nervously from the small veranda. It was only when she got too big and heavy to lift that her father had stopped his game of swinging her around.

But even after the lifting stopped, the gentle hugs and promises of safety had always remained, but sadly those had lasted only until her mother's death.

"Oh Papa," she sighed as she went deeper into the woods. "I don't know what to do to bring you back to your normal senses. I've failed Mama, and I don't know what to do."

The deep silence around her made stop and look around. This was unfamiliar territory, and she then realized that she'd strayed far from her usual path. This was a part of the wood that her father had never once brought her to. He'd warned her over and over again about going too deep into the woods. All manner of dangers lurked out there, and she needed to be careful.

Just as she was turning to go back the way she'd come, she glimpsed part of a wall, and her curiosity overrode any fears within her. Ariel had never met any challenge that she didn't want to overcome and scaling the wall was something she just had to do. There was something beyond the wall and she wanted to find out what it was.

2
THE YEARNING HEART

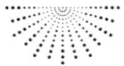

Lord Trevor Welsh, the Duke of Berkeley, stood at the window of his large, empty, and cold manor, staring outside with unseeing eyes. All he could see were patches of snow all over the lawn.

If it had been during summer, the garden just outside his living room would be full of weeds that needed uprooting. He'd not had a gardener for close to three years now because he wanted to be alone. And in three years, he hadn't been back in London either, and couldn't see himself doing so in the foreseeable future.

London held too many painful memories for him, something he didn't like thinking about. Had it been possible, he would have erased a large part of his mind so he wouldn't have to remember all the humiliation he'd suffered when he was last in the capital city. But as it was, memories were like bad recurring dreams. They waited for the moment that a man's defences were down, and then they struck mercilessly and viciously.

Like especially during the holidays when all a person yearned for was family, like he did right now. Three years ago, he'd been looking forward to what he envisioned would be a wonderful marriage with a very beautiful woman. A woman he would have given up everything for, but who turned around and stabbed him so hard in the back that even today, he was still reeling from the shock of the betrayal. And what's more, she'd even seduced his best friend, and they eloped together. But not before they had stolen as much as they could from him, both money and jewellery that his grandmother had left him. And they had left him with deep scars on his face, and one unseeing eye.

But even as he stood at the window, he acknowledged that it wasn't loss of the money and jewellery that hurt him so deeply. It was the fact that for a moment, he'd been deceived into thinking that he would have the loving family he'd always craved. All he had ever wanted from when he was twelve was to have a family of his own. Both of his parents had died in the same year when he turned twelve and he'd had to come and live with his paternal grandparents. But the Duke and Duchess were cold and distant and never showed him any affection. He spent many hours with governesses, and at fourteen, he'd been sent to Eton.

Even among his peers at the prestigious school, Trevor had made very few friends because he was shy and withdrawn, not wanting to draw any attention to himself. It was a great relief when he turned twenty and left school, returning to Berkeley where his grandparents preferred to live.

Percival Wilson was the only friend he let very close to him and they would spend holidays at each other's homes. Cuthbert was the son of an Earl and next in line for the title.

It was his grandmother who had insisted on him meeting young women with the intentions of getting married. The moment his eyes fell on Lady Chloe Mercer, the daughter of Lord Byron Mercer, the Earl of Bedrock, he'd lost his heart to her. He had no idea that Percy had also fallen in love with his fiancée but had held his emotions in check out of respect for Trevor. Sadly, Chloe pitted the two friends against each other, even though she tried to make it as if she were jesting.

It didn't matter to Trevor that the woman got along very well with his grandmother, which should have warned him that she wasn't right for him. But he was too infatuated with her beauty to listen to his inner voice. When she agreed to become his wife, he had believed that all his dreams of having a family would come true. But those dreams turned out to be nothing but fading mists.

He leaned his face against the cold windowpane and sighed deeply. Now that his face was disfigured, he knew that he would never find the kind of love his heart yearned for—the gentle hugs and kisses of a woman who loved him for himself, her sweet smile that would make him feel like he was the most important man in the world.

He and Chloe—and this had occurred to him only recently—had not talked about anything. He'd tried too hard to please first his grandparents and then his betrothed, shutting his eyes to the fact that Chloe had never loved him at all. He was a means to an end, that of gaining a higher title by marriage. He'd convinced himself that love would come later; all they needed to do was get married.

Now he told himself that he would never again beg for a woman's affection like he'd done with his grandmother, and then Chloe. He would never again expose his heart to such pain and anguish. The yearning for love and a family had left him vulnerable to manipulation, and that was a road that he would never travel down again. When he chose to love a woman again, she would have to be someone who needed him as much as he needed her.

Then he groaned out loud, falling to his knees. What was he thinking? What kind of a woman would want to live with a man whose face was so deeply scarred that he was even afraid to look at himself in the mirror?

Even with his deep desire for love and family, where would he find a woman such as the one he yearned for?

Getting over the wall was easy for Ariel as it was overgrown with creeping plants. The stalks were thick enough to hold her weight and she was soon on the other side. Her feet landed in a garden full of weeds and she heard the scurrying of little rodents in the undergrowth.

Looking around her, she noticed an old path that hadn't been used for a while. She made her way to it, treading carefully so she wouldn't slip in the melting snow. Her boots were frayed and full of holes, allowing some sharp plants to prick her feet. She winced but was determined to find out where the path led to.

The wall had surprised her, and she walked for about fifteen minutes and then stopped short. Before her stood an imposing two-story manor, and in the winter sunshine the white walls sparkled. In better days it must have really been beautiful, she thought. Even now it still was, but all the windows seemed to be bolted with planks of wood across them.

Then as she drew even closer to the manor, she noticed something strange. The large front door wasn't completely shut. *Who lived in this deserted manor?* she asked herself as her feet seemed to have a mind of their own and led her right up the ten steps to the door. She tried to peer through the slight gap in the door and then hastily jumped backwards when she heard something like a deep groan coming from within. It sounded like a wounded animal and judging from the deserted look around the house, she wouldn't be surprised if some wild animal crept out of the house. Taking a firm grip on the stick she always carried with her, she once again approached the open door.

The groan sounded again, and she forced herself not to flee even though she was really terrified. Not one to let challenges deter her, Ariel pushed the door open, and its well-oiled hinges made her realize that perhaps this home might not be deserted after all.

The bright and wide foyer was empty, and she stood there for a moment, thinking of how lovely the house looked like inside. The wooden tiles on the floor were in perfect condition even if they didn't seem to have been polished for a while. This was a beautiful house that she longed to explore.

There were three doors leading off the foyer and all stood wide open. A large stairway led to the first floor and she wondered what was up there. She gripped her stick firmly and decided to find out the source of the groaning. The first door she walked through seemed to be the living room and it was large. Most of the furniture was covered with white sheets like it hadn't been used for a while.

As her eyes went around the room, they lighted with shock on the large man who was kneeling with his back towards her. She must have made a sound for he turned, and their eyes met.

Trevor was both shocked and surprised to see a very pretty young woman standing in his living room. For a moment he thought he must have conjured her image and blinked rapidly, even turning away and then back. But she was still there and the look in her eyes was one of curiosity, not revulsion at the scars on his face.

"Sir," she drew even closer, "Are you alright?"

Trevor grunted and slowly rose to his feet. He saw her eyes widen at his large frame.

"The front door was open," she said by way of explanation. "Are you crying?" Trevor was surprised when the lady came even closer to him instead of running away after taking a really good look at his face. "Your eyes are so sad like you're in so much pain," she sat down on one of the few uncovered seats. "Sir, why are you so sad?"

He noticed the stick in her hand and the satchel bag across one arm. Her dressing told him that she was from the village beyond his wall and he wondered how she had managed to enter his estate. Had she come down the driveway, he would have seen her for he'd been standing at the window for a long time.

3

THE UNEXPECTED GUEST

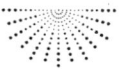

"Who are you and how did you get in here?" Trevor heard the rough rasp in his own voice, signs of long disuse. He couldn't recall the last time he'd had any conversation with anyone. The only person he still communicated with was his solicitor, but through mail and never face to face.

By arrangement with his solicitor, the village grocer dropped supplies for him at the front door on Wednesdays and Saturdays, and he would find his payment under the large rock on the lawn. Trevor always put it there to avoid coming into contact with the man.

From the moment he'd arrived back in his country seat, he'd terminated the services of all the servants, including his personal valet. He didn't want anyone to look at his scarred face and recoil in revulsion. He'd had enough of that with his servants up in London. After the accident, he'd closed up his London house for repairs and even though his solicitor had assured him that it was once again ready for occupation, he'd ignored the man. That was many months ago, and he had no idea if there were any servants left, for he'd asked his solicitor to settle them and then send them all away.

"Who are you?"

"My name is Ariel Dixon and like I said, the front door was open"

"So, Miss Ariel Dixon, do you have the habit of walking through all doors that you find standing open?"

Ariel shrugged, ignoring the growl in his voice. "I heard you groaning and thought that you might be in some kind of trouble, so I came in to check. At first I thought it might be a wild animal but those can't open doors and the hinges were well oiled, so I deduced that it must have been done by a person."

Trevor was speechless for a moment then shook his head. "Did it occur to you that you might be walking into dangerous territory? I could be a bandit hiding in a deserted house."

"Well, are you a bandit hiding in a deserted house?" Ariel demanded and then was surprised to see a smile tagging at the man's lips.

"Where did you come from?"

"I live," she pointed in the direction of the door, "Over the wall, on Lord Charles Fenton's estate. Mama used to make clothes for his servants, so he allowed us to have one of the cottages," she turned red when he raised his eyebrows at her. "I was walking through the woods when I saw the wall. But I didn't see a gate, so I had to climb over it to get here."

"When you see a wall that has no open gate, it means the occupants of that particular compound or estate don't want any intruders or uninvited visitors. That's why people build walls," he said.

Ariel had to tilt her head far back to look up into his face. She observed him through her clear grey eyes, "Are you talking about walls made of bricks and mortar or those imaginary ones around your heart?" Her gaze was unwavering.

Trevor gave a start. This young lady seemed to be seeing right into his soul.

"What do you mean?"

"You look really sad," her eyes wandered around the room. Ariel saw that despite the obvious disrepair, there was evidence that someone had once taken good care of this house. "And yet you have so much," her eyes returned to his. "You have a permanent roof over your head, and I know that your pantry has enough food to feed a whole family. Me," she slowly rose to her feet. "I worry about my Papa all the time. I worry that we won't have rent for the next month. I also worry about what we will eat and the leaking roof on our cottage."

"I'm sorry to hear that, Miss Dixon." Trevor sat down, suddenly feeling overwhelmed.

Ariel noticed that he was looking rather pale. "Sir, can I get you a glass of water?"

"No, I'm alright. Just a little tired, that's all."

"Have you been ill?"

"Not at all, I've always enjoyed good health."

"And that's the reason why you don't have to be sad. Thousands of people would do anything to have what you own right now. It may not look like much, but you need to learn to count your blessings every day. No matter how small the blessing is, just count it and be thankful."

"You make me sound like a total ingrate."

"I didn't say that, but all I mean is that though it's all right to grieve about whatever we've lost, we also have to consider the blessings that God has bestowed upon us," she waved a hand at him. "What is your name?"

A faint smile covered his lips. "Trevor Welsh," he said simply.

The name didn't immediately register in her mind, and then her eyes widened. "The Duke of Berkeley? Are you the duke?"

He chuckled, "I see that you've heard of me."

"Of course, I have. Everyone in Berkeley knows about the duke, but I didn't think you were so young," she took another look at him. "But we all know that the duke lives in London and never comes to Berkeley."

"Well, you're all wrong. This is my country seat, and I live here now. I've been living here for the past three years now."

"But how is it that no one knew you're here? And I thought that a duke's manor would have servants to take care of the house and the garden as well. Don't you have tenants living on your land and how is it that they don't know that you, their master, is in residence at the manor? You seem to live here all alone. If I hadn't seen the door standing slightly ajar, I would never have come in."

"My being here is a long story," Trevor said sadly. "A very long story."

"Why do you choose to live like a recluse? This is a beautiful house and yet you've barred all the windows to keep the light out."

"For a young woman, you sure ask a lot of questions."

"I'm sorry," Ariel blushed. "My Mama used to say that I am like a woodpecker pecking away at things."

"Your mother sounds like a fine woman."

Trevor saw the sadness descending on Ariel's face. "She was a very fine woman, but we lost her last spring. After her death, Papa went to pieces and drinks himself to a stupor every day because of the pain of missing her."

Trevor empathized with the other man. After Chloe had left him, he'd also gone to pieces for a while. First because of the agony of betrayal and then also the physical pain he'd been in after the fire accident.

"I'm very sorry for your loss," he managed to say. "It must be very tough for you to have to deal with double loss."

"What do you mean by double loss? I only lost my Mama. Papa is still alive."

"That may be true but he's absent from you emotionally," then something occurred to him. "How old are you, Miss Dixon."

"I'm seventeen but will turn eighteen in the spring. Why?"

Trevor smiled, "You're still a child even though you have so much to deal with. That has given you a maturity beyond your years. Still, you need to be allowed to enjoy your youthful years."

Ariel shrugged, "My mates, at least some of them, are already married, and some even have little babies now."

"I know that, but it somehow feels all wrong. Why, you and your age mates are barely out of the school room."

Ariel smiled and rose to her feet. "Have you had anything to eat?"

He looked at her in surprise, "Why do you ask?"

"Because I'm hungry and I know that you must be too. I could quickly prepare something for you before I leave."

4
THROUGH THE WALL

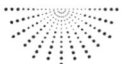

"Don't try to climb over the wall this time, you might fall and hurt yourself," Trevor told Ariel when she was ready to leave. She'd made some eggs, cut them each a thick slice of fresh bread and a cup of tea. It was a simple meal but eating with someone else for a change had made all the difference and Trevor admitted that he'd enjoyed the meal.

"But your gate is too far away for me to use. It will mean practically going to the other side of the village before I can get home."

"Well, this is my estate and I happen to know the small gates that are situated at different points along the wall. They were put there for the servants to use, and when I was young, it was a game of mine to touch all the gates within minutes. Come," he held out a hand and she placed hers in it, trusting him and wondering why she felt so much at ease with this strange man. Well, he wasn't really a stranger because he was the Duke of Berkeley.

It felt so right, and Ariel giggled.

"What now?"

"I can't believe that you've been living out here for nearly three years and no one found out about it. We should have at least seen you when you went down to the village square for groceries."

"That's because I never go to the village square, Miss Dixon. Twice a week, Mr. Lark brings me whatever I need from his store."

"I know that Mrs. Lark, bless her soul, is a good woman but she's also quite the tattle tale. I'm surprised that she's never broadcast your presence in the county to all and sundry abroad."

"That's because her husband was sworn to secrecy," Trevor gave Ariel a sheepish look. "Of course, a few subtle threats were also made, and he hasn't even told his wife about it. He has kept his mouth shut all this while."

She stopped walking forcing him to do the same, "Your grace, why don't you want people to know that you're in the county?"

He touched the tip of her nose with his right index finger. "Your mother was right, you're like a woodpecker, chipping away until you get to the centre of the issue."

"I'm sorry," Ariel thought she had offended her new friend. "I won't ask any more questions." The duke was really nice, and she had enjoyed spending time with him. She'd always been very cautious around strangers and especially men, but Trevor made her feel safe. He made her feel like she was at home and that nothing bad could happen to her while she was with him.

"Ariel, don't look so crestfallen. You've done nothing wrong, and I actually find that curiosity trait that you have quite appealing. But now," he resumed walking. "You need to get home before your father becomes worried about you."

"Pa never worries about me because he is drunk most of the time. But like you say, I need to get home before dark. The woods are eerie in the night and I wouldn't like to get into any kind of trouble."

"I'll walk you part of the way," he said. "Hand me that sack so I can carry it for you."

"It's not that heavy," she protested, thinking about the joint of smoked ham, flour, and half a pound of lard that Trevor had insisted that she take home with her. She was going to prepare a delicious pie for her father. He might not even notice whatever was set before him, but she still had to feed him.

"Well, my grandmother raised me to be a gentleman and not let a lady carry anything while she's in my company." He held out his hand for the sack, and Ariel handed it over. She didn't want to get into any kind of argument with her new friend. "Come, we need to get you home."

Ariel could barely sleep that night. Everything felt like a dream. She'd met the Duke of Berkeley and lived! Then she chuckled softly in the darkness.

While it was true that she'd often speculated about the duke, it had always been more out of a sense of curiosity than anything else. Ariel had long accepted that she was from a lower-class family and her kind didn't mix with nobility.

Nevertheless, whenever she met with her friends, the conversation always turned to the duke and how handsome he was, even though none of them could say for certain that they'd met the man up close. They would talk about how charming the duke was. And like all other starry-eyed teenage girls, each would dream of being asked to a special ball at the large manor, where the duke would fall in love at first sight with one of them, and then together, they would ride off into the sunset. Ariel was no exception, but she'd always thought of the duke as being in his forties. The man who lived in isolation on the walled estate was young, and she guessed that he might be just about thirty or so years old.

Ariel missed her few friends and wished she could find them and share her adventure with them. But she also knew that she must respect Trevor's privacy.

Something had happened to that fine man, and the sadness she'd seen in his blue eyes spoke volumes. What was his story? How had he gotten those terrible scars that marred his otherwise handsome face? And she'd noticed that one of his eyes was funny, like it couldn't see. Even though she'd longed to ask him what had happened to him, she knew it was an invasion of his privacy. Trevor didn't need a busybody trying to dig up painful memories. She would leave matters as they were and not ask about his face or eye. Still, she wished she knew something more about the man.

No one, not even her father knew much about Lord Trevor Welsh because the old duke and duchess had spent ten months of the year in London and only came down to Berkeley during early spring.

They would, of course, hold balls and entertain a lot while they were in the countryside, but only nobles like themselves were invited to such banquets.

Then there was also talk of the duke taking a wife, but again, that would be an affair for the nobility. They all waited for the wedding that never took place, and everyone then assumed that the duke had decided to keep it small and private. Yet all this while, the man had been living in their backyard.

"What happened to you, Trevor?" She murmured, allowing sleep to take over.

On the other side of the county, Lord Welsh was also restless, and he knew that it all had to do with his unexpected visitor that day. He'd never met a woman who was so easy to talk to. Most of those he knew would giggle incessantly and get on his nerves, while fanning themselves with their delicate fans.

But Ariel was real, and he smiled. She was really pretty but still a child, nonetheless. Seventeen to his twenty-seven, and yet she carried herself with a maturity beyond her years. He knew that it all had to do with the cruel hand she'd been dealt.

Had she been the daughter of a nobleman or gentry, she would be getting ready for her coming out season in the spring after she turned eighteen. But Ariel was a little huntress, and he'd chuckled when he noticed the slingshot she had tried so hard to conceal beneath her frayed coat.

She intrigued him, and he made a decision. The village only had one tavern and he was sure that it would be the one place where her father could be found. Donning a thick coat and scarf that concealed most of his face, he left the house on a mission.

He only kept one horse for his personal use, and as he saddled it, thought about the kind of life that he'd created for himself for the past three years. It was lonely and his horse was the only thing he could talk to.

"Well Gus," he murmured, "Let's go out and see the world beyond our high walls." The horse merely snorted.

The tavern was still open even though it was really cold outside. The few candles flickered in the breeze and there were only two patrons seated at separate tables. The tavern owner was dozing at the counter, clearly waiting for his customers to finish their drinks and go home so he could lock up.

"Tell me," he approached the man, "Who are these two men and why are they here so late?"

"That," he pointed, "Is Timothy Dixon and the other is Charles Gate," he finished in bored tones. "It's the night before Christmas Eve and I should have closed up ages ago. I should be seated in front of a merry little fire in my parlour with my sweet wife, sipping warm eggnog. But no," he drawled. "Here I am, waiting on those two drunks who choose to buy the cheapest rum, which isn't even worth my while. And then they take the whole day and night drinking it, as if trying to show others that they, too, can afford alcohol." He tossed the cloth he was holding onto the counter. "I've tried to get them to leave and go home but they're too stubborn to listen to me."

"Does this mean they will be here the whole night then?"

The tavern owner nodded, "Sometimes, I even lock them inside here and go home, but when I come back the next day, they've made a pretty mess of things."

"May I?" Trevor growled deep in his throat.

The tavern keeper shrugged, "Do whatever you want but you'll only be wasting your words with those two."

Trevor chuckled to himself. He had no intention of wasting his words on the two drunkards. They were both of average height and build and no match for him. He first carried the protesting Charles out and tossed him into the snow. Then he returned for Timothy Dixon, who tried to take a swing at him but ended up sprawled flat on his face.

"Stop embarrassing yourself," Trevor told him as he frog-marched the fellow out of the tavern.

"Thank you, Sir, whoever you are. Please pass by any time and have a drink on me," the now happy tavern owner said as he quickly locked up the place.

Charles Gate had staggered off into the night when they got outside. Trevor thought about leaving Tim to do the same, but then Ariel's sweet face came into his mind. She didn't need any more trouble in her life. It looked like the snow might come down again, and he didn't want Timothy buried under it. So, he half dragged, half carried the man and deposited him on his doorstep. He knocked, for he could see that a candle was still burning in one of the rooms, and then melted away into the darkness.

5
BRIGHT NIGHT

Ariel was drifting on the fringes of sleep when she heard heavy footsteps outside their cottage. Heart pounding, she slowly got out of bed and crept toward the cupboard where she pulled out the old rifle she kept there for her own protection.

She didn't like handling guns, but her mother had called it a necessary evil. Most intruders thought twice about confronting someone who was holding a gun, and her father had taught her how to use it. That was the only dangerous venture her mother had agreed to and encouraged.

"We may not always be there to protect our daughter," Margaret Dixon had said. *"And so we have to teach her how to take care of herself."*

The candle in the small parlour was nearly burnt out, and she quickly replaced it with another one. Trevor had given her a handful of them, and she smiled as once again, her thoughts returned to him. He really was a kind and generous man.

She thought she heard something like a grunt outside the door and at first thought it was a wild pig that had strayed from the woods, for they sometimes did that.

"Who is there?" she asked in a fearful voice but at first only silence greeted her words. Then she heard her father's drunken voice as he broke out into one of his favourite ballads and her heart settled down. Putting the rifle aside, she opened the door and slipped her hands under his armpits and dragged him in.

"Oh Papa! What am I going to do with you?"

She noticed that he didn't have a bottle in his hand and like he usually did. And she was surprised that he'd come in earlier than usual. He usually staggered home after the first cock had crowed and sometimes never.

"Papa, you're breaking my heart," she wept as she dumped him on the floor and locked the door securely. "Do you want to die and leave me all alone in this world? I promised Mama that I would always take care of you, but now I don't know what to do."

Timothy hiccupped and continued with his drunken singing. "Get me my bottle," he said as she dragged him to the room.

"There's no more drink."

"Get my bottle," he said and lashed out, the blow catching her on the side of the head. She went backwards reeling and struck her head on the wall, and everything went dark for a few seconds.

When she regained her senses and picked herself up from the floor, her father had fallen face first across the bed and was snoring.

Her cheek and head hurt but she dashed the tears away and stood looking down at her father.

"Oh Pa, you're really breaking my heart," she carried the candle out of her father's bedroom and returned to her own. What was she going to do with her father?

∼

The first thing Trevor noticed when Ariel came to the manor the next day was that she had a scarf around her head and it covered her face. Even though it was a chilly morning, for it had snowed heavily in the night, he expected her to take the scarf off once she entered the house.

For the first time in a long while, he'd gone to the shed at the back of the house and chopped up enough wood for a merry fire. And he'd also found himself humming as he cleaned up the living room in anticipation of his visitor.

Ariel looked quite pale, and he frowned. This wasn't the same cheerful young woman he'd met the previous day. Something was definitely wrong.

"Ariel," he called out softly, startling her. "What's wrong?"

"Nothing," she mumbled, lowering herself on the couch and bowed her head.

"I know it was chilly outside, but you can take the scarf off now."

She shook her head, feeling a little lightheaded.

Trevor came and crouched before her and reached for the scarf, but her fingers tightened around it.

"In a game of pitting strength against each other, we both know what the outcome will be," he said in his deep quiet voice. With a swift tag, he pulled the scarf off and then stared at the bruise on her cheek. It had turned purple and looked really ugly.

"Who did this to you, Ariel?" the sound was like a deep growl and she felt frightened. "Ariel, who hurt you?"

"He didn't mean to do it," she said in a soft voice, tears filling her eyes.

"Did your father do this to you?" He rose to his feet and sat down next to her, pulling her until she was on his lap. "I'm so sorry."

No one had showed her such kindness and tenderness time since her mother's death months ago and Ariel cuddled up to his chest and wept.

"Hush, my little one," Trevor said over and over again, gently stroking her hair until the weeping died down.

"I'm sorry," Ariel hiccoughed.

"Child, you've been carrying a very heavy load for a long while now. But you'll be all right, for you are a strong young woman, Ariel." He gently got her off his lap and back onto the couch. "Now tell me what really happened."

She twisted her fingers nervously. "Pa didn't mean to hit me."

"Just tell me what happened," he insisted, and she did so in halting terms.

"Has this ever happened before?" She turned her face away and he had his answer. "I see," he said.

"Please," Ariel turned her watery eyes to him. "My father is a good man. Mama's death hit him hard because they were so much in love. And he wasn't always a drunkard. I know that one day he'll come back to his senses."

"Well," Trevor said with controlled emotions. "You're all right now." It was clear she loved her father and would defend him at all times, even when he was abusive toward her. But dwelling on the subject was upsetting to her. So he decided to get off the topic, at least for the moment. "Ariel, I notice that you speak like one who received some form of education; did you have a governess or something?"

She shook her head, glad that he was off the topic about her father.

"Mama was a seamstress, and she made clothes for the baron's servants. Baroness Catherine insisted that those working in her household should be cultured, as she liked to put it. So, Mama had to learn how to speak like the other servants, and she would teach me also."

"You mother must have been a very remarkable woman."

"She was," Ariel felt the tears returning but rapidly blinked them away. "I caught a rabbit and wanted to prepare some stew for you."

"You're a very fascinating young woman," Trevor got to his feet. "Where is it?"

"I hid it in the bushes outside the house," she jumped to her feet. "Let me get it," and before he could say anything else, she'd darted out of the house.

She returned with her trophy and made her way to his large kitchen. He followed her slowly and watched as she skilfully skinned and dressed the rabbit. She then skewered it and set it over the fire in the heath.

"It amazes me that in large houses such as this one, the fire never dies down," Ariel said, breaking the silence that was stretching out her nerves. The duke's gaze was unnerving especially because he just sat at the kitchen table watching her as she worked.

"Ariel, you don't have to be nervous around me."

"I know," she gave him a sheepish grin.

"Good. Now, will you be all right on your own for a little while? I want to ride out to the village square to attend to some business."

"Don't you mind that people will see you?"

He smiled, "They have to see me sometime," and inwardly he added that the most important person to him didn't care about the scars on his face or the fact that he didn't have vision in one eye. But he didn't voice that thought out loud.

"I need to get my valet back, and also make arrangements for the other servants to come back to work."

"You want to reopen the house?"

"Yes," he smiled gently at her, and Ariel completely lost her heart to him in that moment.

"I'll lock the front door. Make sure you don't open up for anyone until I get back. And also, feel free to explore the house even though later when we have the time, I'll give you a more extensive tour of the place."

"Thank you."

He walked toward the door and then returned. "You have very expressive eyes, and I know you want to know what happened to my face."

"No ..."

"Ariel, the one thing I can't really stand from those around me is lies. Now, do you want me to tell you what happened to me?"

"Your Grace ..."

"No matter, I'll tell you more when I get back. Remember, don't open the door for anyone unless it's me."

"Yes, Your Grace."

∽

After visiting his much-surprised valet at the man's home, Trevor made his way to the tavern which was almost empty since it was mid morning. But the man he sought was already seated at a table and from the still-full bottle, it was clear that he hadn't started drinking yet.

"Timothy Dixon," he said as he slid into the chair across from Ariel's father. Timothy's eyes widened in recognition. "Yes, I can see that you have recognized me since you're not yet drunk." Trevor leaned forward so the conversation would be private. "Let me give you just one final warning. I'm the duke of this county, and I expect my people to adhere to certain standards of conduct. Drunkenness isn't one of them and you should consider yourself warned. If you ever lay a finger on your beautiful daughter again...."

"Who, Ariel?" The man looked slightly confused. "I would never lay a finger on my daughter."

"Sane and sober, you wouldn't. But when you get drunk, you lose control of yourself and strike her. Mr. Dixon, I won't repeat this warning to you again. If I ever hear that you've laid a finger on your daughter again, you'll rue the day you became a citizen of this county. Do I make myself clear?"

Timothy cowered at the violence he sensed in the other man. "It was all an accident."

"You've got a lot going for you," Trevor said with a growl. "A home and a daughter who loves you so much that she risks her life for you every day. What sort of a father are you? Do you know that a father is supposed to protect and provide for his offspring? Yet you leave that innocent and vulnerable girl to fend for herself. It's just a matter of time before some unscrupulous character takes advantage of your drunkenness and attacks that poor child. Do you know how many dangers your daughter is exposed to everyday as she goes hunting in the woods just to make sure there's food on the table and a roof over your heads? What if you one day come home drunk as usual and find that someone has attacked your daughter and ravished her? Is that what you want for your child? And what would your beloved wife say if she were to return and see the harm you're doing to her beautiful girl?" Trevor's eyes were blazing. "Like I said, I won't repeat this conversation with you ever again. Consider yourself warned," and he swiftly rose to his feet, tossed a gold guinea to the happy tavern owner and left.

Oswald, his old valet, had promised to recruit some servants, but they would be coming by the house on the twenty-seventh. It was Christmas Eve after all, and everyone needed to be with their families.

He mounted his horse, a smile on his face, and was unaware of the dashing picture he made as he rode back home to the beautiful young woman who was waiting for him. And he left tongues wagging as he tipped his hat at his stunned citizens.

Even the sun peeped through the clouds to smile upon the day.

Ariel had just finished serving the rabbit when she thought she heard a carriage at the front door. As far as she knew, Trevor had gone out on horseback and she wondered if perhaps he might have decided to get himself a carriage.

The large knocker sounded, and she knew it couldn't be Trevor. He would have come through the back. His warning rang in her mind and she stayed right where she was, heart pounding. *Who could have decided to pay the duke a visit on a day such as this one?* she wondered.

Just as she was nervously twisting her hands, she heard someone riding up to the back door and a few minutes later there was a soft knock. "Ariel, it's me."

She ran to the door and unbolted it, letting the duke in. "There's someone at the front door."

"I know," his lips tightened. He'd recognized the carriage. "Stay here and let me deal with whoever it is."

Ariel thought he was acting oddly, but she simply nodded and went back to whatever she was doing.

Trevor watched her bent head for a brief moment then walked out of the kitchen and to the front door to open it.

"Oh Trevor, my love," Chloe stood outside his door. "Aren't you going to let me in?"

"Forgive my manners, Lady Chloe, but I don't understand what you're doing here. Where is your husband?"

"I left him in Paris and decided to come and see you."

"Why?" He was truly curious. Now that he'd gotten over her, he wondered what he'd seen in her in the first place. "It's not proper for a lady to be alone in a man's house. People might not understand."

"Oh Trevor," he saw tears well up in her eyes, "I realise that I made a terrible mistake."

"What sort of a mistake did you make?"

"Please allow me to come in," she pulled her gloves off. "It's not proper for my groomsmen to see me standing out here."

"Very well then," Trevor opened the door and allowed her in.

"This place looks dismal. What have you done to it, Trevor?" Chloe touched the surfaces. "There's dust all over the place," she grimaced. "Where are the servants?"

"I don't have any," Trevor followed her into the living room. "What do you want, Chloe."

"Trevor," she came close to him, but he put her away. "You know that I never stopped loving you."

He gave her a sad smile, "You really had a fine way of showing your love to me."

"I made a terrible mistake and I'm sorry."

"Well, I forgave you a long time ago because I realised that being bitter at you and Percy was only harming me." He looked at her. "Why can't you look at me in the face, Chloe?" This he said because he saw her avoiding direct eye contact with him. "These scars," he touched his face, "Will never fade and I can't see with my left eye. Why are you here Chloe, when you made it so obvious that Percy was your choice?"

~

Ariel was curious about who the visitor was, and she tiptoed toward the living room to find out. She didn't want Trevor to know she was eavesdropping on the conversation. From the open door, she saw a very beautiful woman who was well adorned.

"We were engaged to be married, Trevor. Please don't do this to me."

"Lady Chloe, I'm not doing anything to you. You were the one who chose to run away with my best friend while I lay in pain after the accident you caused."

"Trevor, it was an accident. I didn't mean to drop the candle on the drapes as you were sleeping."

"I don't want to go back to that terrible day when I nearly died," he turned away from her, fighting for control. "I was badly injured and when I regained consciousness, the first thing my valet told me was that my money and the jewellery my grandmother had left me was missing. And you were gone. Imagine my astonishment when my man brought me the newspaper and I saw your engagement and then marriage to my best friend."

"It was a terrible mistake, and you know that Percy was the one who made me do it. He was always jealous of you, but he's not even half the man you are, Trevor."

"Listen, Chloe, three years ago, I would have taken you back at the drop of a hat. But now ..." he shook his head, "A lot had happened in this time that we've been apart, and unlike Percy, I would never betray my best friend like this. You need to leave before your servants begin to talk."

"I came here to be with you, Trevor. This can be our own little secret."

He threw his head back and laughed, "Dear woman, you really must be out of your mind to imagine that I would do something as heinous as to get involved with a married woman."

"We're all alone in this house," she said triumphantly, "I'll tell people that you overpowered me and ravished me."

"Sadly, no one will believe you because that's not my character, and besides, we're not alone in the house," Trevor said. Ariel crept back to the kitchen and a few minutes later, heard footsteps. "My love," Trevor came into the kitchen and walked straight towards her. He took her in his arms and kissed her soundly. "Please meet Countess Chloe, my best friend's wife." He turned to Chloe, "This is my beautiful wife, Ariel. Now, if there's nothing more, would you please excuse us? We were about to sit down and have our lunch."

Chloe gave Ariel a scathing look. "I see that you've lowered your standards, Trevor." There was a contemptuous sneer on her face. "You picked a village girl and married her? What will the whole of London say when they get to hear of this?"

Trevor shrugged, "I don't really care what London says because I haven't been there in three years. You made sure of that, Chloe. And down here, no one really cares who I marry."

"This is low even for you, Trevor."

"If you'll please excuse us," he kissed Ariel's forehead and then took Chloe's elbow, firmly walking her out of the kitchen and house and to her carriage. "My regards to dear old Percy," he bowed and without waiting to see if she had stepped into the carriage, he walked back up the steps and shut the door.

Ariel was wringing her hands nervously when he walked back into the kitchen. "She's very beautiful."

"Very true, dear child. But true beauty comes from within and not from what is visible to the eye. Now, shall we partake of our lunch?"

"I already served it." Ariel said. "I'd like to go home now."

"Why? Did I do or say something that upset you?"

She shook her head, "I need to go and prepare my father's meal."

"Ariel, please sit down," he pointed at the chair opposite his. "What's wrong?"

"I shouldn't be here, for people will talk. What if the countess goes and tells people that she found us alone in the house? They will think that my virtue has been compromised."

"In that case then I'll have to marry you," he smiled, and to her consternation, she burst into tears and ran out of the kitchen, forgetting her satchel and stick. She ignored him as he tried to call her back and ran toward the small gate in the wall. She knew that he couldn't run as fast, and once she was out of the estate, she paused and took a deep breath.

Trevor knew that he'd said the wrong thing to Ariel as soon as the words left his lips. She might be a village girl, but she was very intelligent and his careless mention of marriage was regrettable.

6

A CHANGED MAN

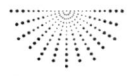

"Papa are you alright?" Ariel was surprised when she got home and found her father already there. It was much too early for him to be at home, and he was seated on the wooden couch on the small veranda he'd constructed for her mother years ago. And wonder of wonders, he wasn't drunk at all. "Papa?" She came and sat next to him. "Please talk to me."

He turned sad eyes to her. "I really miss her," his voice broke.

"Pa," Ariel put an arm around him and leaned on his shoulder. "I miss her so much, too."

"And I've wronged you terribly, Ariel, my child." He took her hand. "On the day your mother died, you lost not one parent but both of us. I've failed you, and I'm so sorry."

"Papa, I'm just glad that you're now well," she wiped her tears. "My Pa is back." She refused to dwell on the pain in her heart as she paid attention to her father. "I'm truly surprised to find you here at this time."

"And I promise that I'll be here to take care of you from now on."

"We'll take care of each other."

"Your mother would have been so proud to see the kind of woman you've become, Ariel. I know we lost her just a few months ago, but in that time, you've grown up so much, and I'm so proud of you."

"Thank you, Pa. Now let me go in and prepare us something for our dinner. It's Christmas Eve after all and we need a meal that's fit for a king." There was still some pie left over from their previous meal, and she went to the kitchen to prepare it. She needed time alone to think about Trevor.

She called herself all kinds of a fool for falling in love with a man who was way beyond her class. He was a duke, for crying out loud, and she a common villager. Chloe had said it, and in that moment that the three of them had been standing in the kitchen, she'd seen the vast class difference between them. She'd been living a dream, but meeting the countess had finally opened her eyes.

Trevor might live like a recluse, but he was still a duke.

∼

He was in love and he was doomed. Trevor paced the corridors of the manor wondering what he was going to do about all these feelings that threatened to overwhelm him. He'd never felt this way about anyone before, not even Chloe. And now that he thought about it, what he'd felt for his runaway fiancée was nothing more than foolish boyish infatuation. Even though he was angry that she had come to the house and caused problems between him and Ariel, he was glad that it had happened. For one, it had proved to him that he was finally over her, and he also got to find out the kind of woman he'd nearly married. It was clear that she was bored with her marriage, and he wondered if she and Percy had any children. Since he never read the newspapers, hadn't done so for three years, he had no idea of what had been happening in the world out there. And his solicitor, good man that he was, had never once mentioned Chloe or Percy in any of the letters they'd exchanged. But one thing was for sure, he was completely over his foolish infatuation with Chloe.

What he felt for Ariel, however, was something that touched his heart, soul, and spirit. She had taken over his heart, and he knew that she would never leave.

But Ariel was ten years younger than he was—not even out of her teens. She was a child/woman and he felt guilty just thinking about her in a romantic way. He wasn't one of those men who found satisfaction in running after small girls. He knew that some of his peers went after girls as young as fourteen years old and saw nothing wrong with that, but not him.

She'd run out of the house in anger and hurt, and much as he wanted to go after her, he knew that he needed to give her time. Would she come by the house tomorrow? Had he messed up any chance of love with her?

"Oh Ariel," he groaned as he leaned against the balustrade and stared down into the foyer. It was because of her that he'd decided to bring life back to his manor. But did she feel anything for him at all?

They had spent two days together, and he knew that he loved her deeply. But he was also realistic enough to know that love between them would never work. Not because of the class difference, but because of her age.

7
IS THIS LOVE

It had to be a Christmas miracle, Ariel thought as she prepared breakfast for her and her father. For the first time in months, he wasn't drunk.

She could hear him whistling at the back of the house while he chopped up some more wood for them to use. She couldn't remember the last time he'd done any chores around the house. And he wasn't whistling one of his drunken songs, it was actually one of the ones her mother had liked singing.

"Papa, breakfast is ready," she called out as she served the remaining piece of pie. They each got a slice.

Timothy entered the house, wiping his hands on his trouser. "Ariel," he stared at the feast that was laid out on his small table, "We've feasted like nobility these past two days, where did all this food come from? Is the baron back?"

"Papa, please sit down and don't ask me too many questions. Merry Christmas to you, Pa."

"Merry Christmas to you too," he smiled as he took his seat. They enjoyed the sumptuous meal and apart from her mother's absence, things were back as before.

"Pa, I'm going to hunt for some duck for our Christmas dinner. Will you be alright?"

"Yes, my child. But you should wait until I'm done fixing the roof then we can go hunting together."

"That won't be necessary, Pa. You know that the woods are teeming with folks also looking for Christmas dinner. If we delay, we won't catch anything. Don't worry, I'll be alright, Pa."

∽

Trevor woke up with a sense of foreboding. He felt quite dejected and sighed as he sat up in his large bed. Then he recalled the events of the day before and groaned, covering his face with his palms. Would Ariel come by today or was she still angry with him?

She deserved to be treated better than he'd done and he would wait for some time for her. If she didn't show up, he would go by her house and apologise to her. She might not want to have anything to do with him and he wouldn't blame her. He'd made her feel like she didn't matter and that made his stomach churn.

But perhaps it was all for the best since he was much older than her. She deserved to fall in love with a young man, not him. And even though it would break his heart to see her go, he loved her enough to want her to find true love and happiness.

"Oh Ariel," he groaned as he staggered out of the bedroom, robe untied. The belt hung down on both sides and he shuffled barefooted across to the stairs. He badly needed a drink of water first and then he would return to wait for Ariel. If she wasn't here by lunch time, he'd go to their cottage and apologise, then walk away from her.

As he got to the stairs, he missed a step and before he could reach out a hand to break his fall, he went tumbling down the stairs and lay at the bottom in an unconscious heap.

∼

Ariel didn't want to go to the manor because she was still hurting from yesterday. But it was Christmas Day and her mother had always told her that one should never go to bed angry. She'd gone to bed angry and woken up sad.

After wrestling with her thoughts for a while, she decided to go and see Trevor just to get things sorted out between them. She would then tell him that she could no longer come by his house because she didn't want to create a situation where he would be forced to offer marriage just to save her name. A marriage based on that would never work and they would soon become resentful of each other.

Walking away with a broken heart was better than allowing a terrible situation to arise. Even if the duke found himself forced to marry her, he would never treat her as an equal because she was a mere village girl.

When Ariel got to the house, she frowned as she tried the front door and found it still locked. She walked round the house to the back and the kitchen door was also locked. But there was a window in the pantry that she could squeeze into and after dropping the two ducks she was carrying inside, she scrambled in, careful not to step on them.

Trevor usually woke up early and went riding. She'd noticed that the stable door was still bolted from the outside and finding both house doors still locked meant that something was wrong, and the eerie silence that met her entrance into the house frightened her.

"Your Grace," she called out and heard her voice echoing in the large house. "Trevor?"

Once more, silence greeted the echo of her voice and her heart started pounding. What if he'd been taken ill in the night?

She tossed the two ducks she'd caught onto the kitchen table and rushed out, coming to a dead stop when she saw the love of her life lying on the floor at the foot of the stairs.

"Trevor," she was immediately at his side and on her knees, sobbing as she felt for a pulse. Finding none at first, she started rubbing his chest.

"Trevor, please don't die and leave me," she sobbed. "What will happen to me now? I love you and can't live without you, Trevor. Please open your eyes. I'm not angry with you anymore, please just wake up. You're the only one who has ever showed me so much kindness and love, please don't leave me."

Trevor heard the weeping as if from afar and struggled with the cloud of darkness that was trying to hold him down. He felt the soft kisses on his face.

"I love you, Trevor. If you die on me, I'll be very cross with you. Open your eyes and wipe my tears away," she demanded.

He raised his hand and touched Ariel's face, "I'm not dead," he whispered, and she gave a cry of joy and fell across his chest.

"Ariel!" She quickly turned to see her father staring down at them. "What's going on here?"

"Oh Pa, I thought my Trevor was dead," she said, laughing and crying at the same time. "I found him lying at the bottom of the stairs. Quick, help me get him to the couch. Pa, don't just stand there," she ordered and Trevor chuckled softly. The love of his life was quite a formidable little woman.

They soon had him on the couch, and she ran up the stairs to get him a blanket.

"What are you doing here, Mr. Dixon?" He struggled to sit up and winced at the pain in his head.

"I got suspicious when my girl wouldn't let me go hunting with her, so I followed her. She caught two ducks, and when she didn't immediately make for home, I knew she was up to something. Your Grace, what are your intentions toward my daughter?"

8
LOVE AT LAST

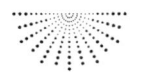

Christmas lunch had been served and eaten and everyone was replete. But Trevor still had some issues to take care of.

"Mr. Dixon?"

"Yes, Your Grace."

"It would be an honour if you will grant me permission to ask you for your daughter's hand in marriage."

"What?"

"Yes, Sir," Trevor looked at Ariel with so much love in his eyes that her father was left in no doubt that this man genuinely adored his daughter.

"Ariel?" Was all he asked, and the two men looked at her.

"Papa?"

"The man just asked for your hand in marriage. What do you have to say?"

"Is it up to me?" She stared at her father with an incredulous expression on her face.

"Yes, my child, Ariel. Your mother made me promise that when it came to love, you would make your own choice. I was to only make sure that the man is a good person," he looked at the duke solemnly. "I haven't heard any scandals attached to this man's name and from what I can see, he genuinely loves you."

Ariel raised her eyes to Trevor and saw a deep vulnerability in his. She really loved this man but there was still the class difference that stood like a wall between them. Would society ever accept a marriage between a nobleman and a common village girl.

"Your Grace," she bit her lower lip nervously, "We don't belong in the same class. The Countess pointed that out yesterday, and it's all true."

"Ariel," Trevor reached out a hand and she placed hers in it. "Please marry me and share my class. Marry me, and my class will become yours too. Marry me, and we will be of the same class."

"But what will people say?"

"I don't care what people say, Ariel. All I know is that I love you so strongly, and that's something I can't explain. A few days ago, I was here alone and in deep despair. You see, the Countess and I were engaged, but three years ago, she set fire to the curtain in my bedroom while I was asleep. Whether it was intentional or by accident, I have no idea. Chloe said she'd dropped the candle by mistake. That was how I got these scars and also lost sight in my left eye," he shrugged, "But that's all in the past. Yes, Chloe is a beautiful and titled woman, but she doesn't have the kind of heart that I want."

"What kind of heart do you want?"

"A pure heart filled with true love," he smiled tenderly at her. "A heart that beats like mine, with all honesty and sincerity in it. I'll certainly not be the first duke to marry a woman who isn't of the nobility, and in no way will I be the last. Love doesn't choose where it falls, and since I have the final say in what happens in my own life, I want to marry you, Ariel. Will you have me?"

She was silent for a while, and Trevor felt nervous. He turned his eyes to her father, appealing for his intervention.

"Girl, put the man out of his misery. Do you love him or not?"

Ariel thought about the sacrifice Trevor was willing to make in order to marry her. He would be ridiculed and laughed at, but he didn't seem like the kind of man to care what others said. And he'd chosen her over Chloe, which meant a lot to her. Yes, this was the kind of man that she wanted to spend the rest of her life with. So, she gave him a sweet smile.

"Yes, Papa. I love Trevor."

"He's a duke."

She snorted, a very unladylike sound that warmed the heart of her beloved. "Pa, even if he is a duke, he's still the love of my life."

EPILOGUE

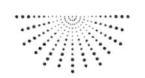

New Year's Day 1816

The wedding between the Duke of Berkeley and one little common village girl would be talked about for years to come. First, because it was quite lavish, and guests came in from as far as London. Word had gone round that Lord Trevor was back from overseas, for that was what the tabloids said, and he'd retired to his country seat to recuperate after injuries suffered in the war.

Of course, it was just a rumour, but the duke's solicitor took advantage of that to win favours for his client. It was also the reason why the solicitor was able to obtain a special licence for them immediately. No one could refuse the request of a wartime hero.

To Lord Welsh, however, nothing mattered to him except that the love of his life, the true one this time, had agreed to become his wife.

The wedding took place at the newly opened up manor, and all the good citizens of Berkeley Duchy were invited to the joyous occasion.

Never had they seen such large tables that groaned under the weight of stacks of delicacies. Everyone ate to their fill.

"Are you happy, my darling?" Trevor couldn't believe that he finally held his woman in his arms. He could hear music and laughter outside, and the sun had decided to melt the snow and give them a really pleasant day. But after all the pomp and glory, Ariel had begged him to take her to the study so she could get away from all the noise for a short moment.

"Trevor," she snuggled close to him. "I love you so much and I'm so happy. But it's going to take me time to get used to your friends from London. I'm very nervous around them."

"Don't be; they're just human like we are. Besides, I was sure to invite only those who are close enough to me and who don't judge others based on which side of the road they were born. That's why our guest list of those from London was very short."

"Will you ever take me to London to see the Regent Prince?"

He chuckled softly, "If that's what you want, my darling. For you, I would cross the ocean in a teacup paddling with a teaspoon," he winked at her.

She giggled, "That's a very silly analogy but I like it. Will you teach me how to be a lady so that I won't ever embarrass you in front of your friends?"

"That's the reason Miss Denison was employed. She was my old governess and I know that the two of you will get along very well. She's also very kind and will treat you with much respect."

"Thank you and I promise that I'll be a good student."

"Well, for this first year, I want you all to myself so we will remain here in the countryside. During this time, you'll take your lessons with Miss Denison and come next year, we shall move to London."

"What if I don't like London that much?"

"Then we'll come back here and make our own fairytale kind of life, my darling," he kissed her full on the lips. "You have brought sunshine into my life. I received my Christmas miracle on the day you walked into this house, and now the New Year begins with so much joy for us."

"This indeed has been a great miracle," Ariel agreed. "I had been dreading Christmas because Mama was not with us, but I didn't know that Pa and I would receive such a great blessing. You've really changed our lives and I love you so much for it."

Trevor had put his father-in-law to be in charge of his stables because Ariel told him that Timothy loved horses. And there was a nice comfortable cottage that had been prepared for him. Work was still ongoing to restore the vast estate, but the duke knew that he had capable men working for him.

"It will always be a pleasure of mine to make you happy, my Duchess, because I love you so much, too."

As the wedding guests continued celebrating outside, the two lovers held each other as they watched the fire that was burning merrily in the grate. They had found love; they had found forever with each other.

∼

THANK YOU FOR CHOOSING A PUREREAD BOOK!

We hope you enjoyed the story, and as a way to thank you for choosing PureRead we'd like to send you this free book, and other fun reader rewards…

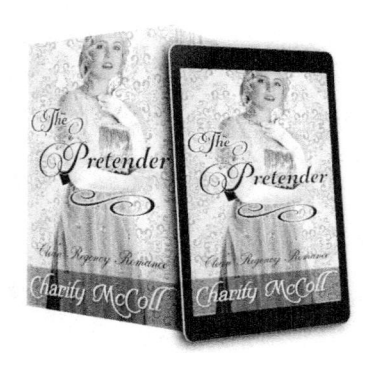

An undercover plan designed to win a young nobleman's heart is threatened when the lovely Gabrielle Belgrade's soft conscience and honesty threatens to undo the matchmaking shenanigans of Lord Grant's well intentioned godmother.

Click here for your free copy of The Pretender
PureRead.com/regency

Thanks again for reading.
See you soon!

OUR GIFT TO YOU

AS A WAY TO SAY THANK YOU WE WOULD LOVE TO SEND YOU THIS BEAUTIFUL STORY FREE OF CHARGE.

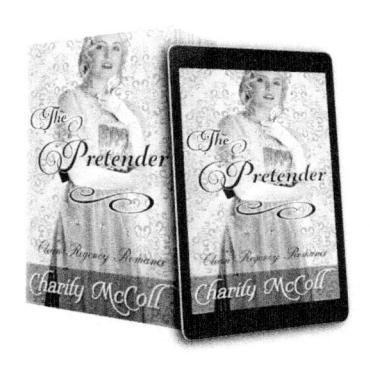

An undercover plan designed to win a young nobleman's heart is threatened when the lovely Gabrielle Belgrade's soft conscience and honesty threatens to undo the matchmaking shenanigans of Lord Grant's well intentioned godmother.

Click here for your free copy of The Pretender

PureRead.com/regency

At PureRead we publish books you can trust. Great tales without smut or swearing, but with all of the mystery and romance you expect from a great story.

Be the first to know when we release new books, take part in our fun competitions, and get surprise free books in your inbox by signing up to our free VIP Reader list.

As a thank you you'll receive a copy of *The Pretender* straight away in you inbox.

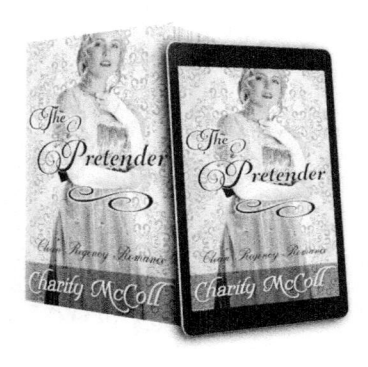

Click here for your free copy of The Pretender

PureRead.com/regency

Printed in Great Britain
by Amazon